*This book
belongs to*

The
Busy
Baker

AND OTHER SILLY STORIES

The Busy Baker

AND OTHER SILLY STORIES

PARRAGON

First published in Great Britain in 1998 by
Parragon
13 Whiteladies Road
Clifton
Bristol BS8 1PB

Copyright © Parragon 1998

ISBN 0 75252-533-6

Printed in Great Britain

Reprinted in 1999

Produced by Nicola Baxter
PO Box 71
Diss Norfolk IP22 2DT

Stories by Nicola Baxter
Designed by Amanda Hawkes
Text illustrations by Duncan Gutteridge
Cover illustration by Alisa Tingley

Contents

The Busy
Baker

Once upon a time, there was a very busy baker. He was busy because his bread and cakes and biscuits were the most delicious for miles around. If a person tasted just one of them, he or she would never want to eat anything made by another baker again.

The baker made bread that smelled heavenly and tasted so good that some people ate it just by itself without cheese or jam or honey.

The baker made cakes that melted in your mouth and made you wish you could eat them for breakfast, lunch *and* supper.

The baker made biscuits that were the crispest and crumbliest you have ever tasted. Many an important person in the town walked around with telltale crumbs on his waistcoat!

But it wasn't only because his baking was popular that the baker was so busy. The fact was that he was never satisfied with the wonderful things he made. He always had to be trying something to improve them, or working hard to invent a recipe that had never been made before.

So the baker worked night and day. His chimney could be seen smoking at midnight, and he was up again to make bread for the morning by three o'clock.

Of course, it is much easier to work hard at something you like than it is to put a lot of effort into a job you hate. But the baker was only human, and no one can go without sleep or rest or holidays for ever. It was inevitable that sooner or later, the baker would make a mistake.

This is how it happened. One day in early summer, a lady who lived very near the baker took her little niece into the bakery to choose a cake for her tea. The little girl's mummy was rather ill, which was why Anna-Maria was

staying with her aunty. It was also why her aunty was trying to be specially nice to the little girl, although, to be honest, that was not always easy. Perhaps it was because she was worried about her mummy, but Anna-Maria was often a very difficult child.

As they stood looking at the wonderful selection of cakes and biscuits, Mrs Biddle (for that was the aunt's name) urged her niece to make her choice.

"I know they *all* look delicious," she said, "but you must choose just one of them. We can always come back tomorrow so that you can try something else."

But Anna-Maria looked at the lovely cakes and scowled.

"I can't see anything I want," she said.

"But darling," cried Mrs Biddle, "there is everything you could imagine here. Look! What about a doughnut? What about a cream horn? Or you could have a chocolate muffin, or a jam slice, or a coconut swirl."

"No," said Anna-Maria. "That's not what I want."

Mrs Biddle tried again.

"A coffee kiss? A currant bun? A cinnamon plait?"

"No," said the little girl.

"What about a slice from one of these beautiful *big* cakes? There's a lemon sponge. Or look, a cherry loaf. A chocolate-chip log? A carrot cake? A double-decker date and walnut wonder?"

But Anna-Marie frowned again and shuffled her shoes.

"I don't like anything here," she muttered sullenly.

Mrs Biddle had plenty of patience. She needed it all now.

"Well, what *do* you like?" she asked. "The baker may well have some other cakes at the back, where we can't see them."

"Yes, that's true," smiled the baker. "What would the little lady really like?"

Mrs Biddle had told the baker about Anna-Maria's mother, so he too wanted to be kind to the little girl.

And Anna-Maria did know just what she wanted.

"I'd like a gingerbread man, please," she said, quite politely.

The busy baker's chubby cheeks looked a little pink.

"I'm very sorry," he said. "I'm afraid I haven't made any of those for a long time. My new gingerbread teddy bears rather took over, you know. Wouldn't you like one of those?"

"No, thank you," said Anna-Maria. "It has to be a gingerbread man, please."

"Well, I haven't any now," said the smiling baker, "but I will make some tonight specially for you. They will be ready first thing in the morning."

For the first time, Anna-Maria smiled. "Oh, *thank* you!" she cried. "That will be lovely!"

What neither Mrs Biddle nor the baker knew was that the little girl's mother made her gingerbread men on special occasions. Anna-Maria thought that perhaps she would not miss her mummy quite so much if she had a gingerbread man just like the ones she loved at home.

That night, the busy baker had to work even harder than usual, and perhaps that is why he didn't pay quite as much attention to what he was doing as he should have done.

The next morning, Mrs Biddle and her niece called at the shop only five minutes after it had opened for the day.

"Here you are, sweetheart," smiled the busy baker. "Six little gingerbread men, just for you."

Anna-Maria looked down at the little biscuits in their special box. They were lovely, but her face fell as she glanced at them.

"What's the matter, darling?" asked Mrs Biddle. "Is there something wrong?"

The little girl looked up with tears in her eyes.

"They haven't got any buttons!" she said.

"What? Let me look!" cried the baker, taking back the box. "Oh dear, oh dear, you are quite right. They really *should* have buttons, shouldn't they?"

"Currant buttons," said Anna-Maria firmly.

"Yes, yes, that's just what I was thinking," said the baker, looking a little embarrassed. "I'm so sorry. If you come back tomorrow, I'll make sure I have gingerbread men with buttons. I was thinking of three buttons. Would that be right?"

"That would be just right," said Anna-Maria, for her mother's special gingerbread men always had three currant buttons.

That night, the baker worked hard again. In fact, he was so busy making sure there were buttons on his biscuits that the bread was left to rise for too long and almost burst out of the oven.

Next morning, Anna-Maria and her aunty were waiting outside the shop when the baker opened the door.

"I've got them right here," he smiled. "And I counted the buttons very carefully."

Anna-Maria's blue eyes were bright as she peered into the box. There was a little smile on her lips. But suddenly her eyes clouded and she almost looked ready to cry.

"Whatever is it now?" asked Mrs Biddle. "They look lovely to me, sweetheart."

"But they don't have red smiley mouths," said Anna-Maria.

It was perfectly true. The jolly gingerbread men had little currant eyes and little currant buttons, but in his concern to make sure there were exactly three buttons on each little man, the busy baker had completely forgotten about the red smiley mouths made from cherries.

"Oh dear," said the baker, "I'm not doing very well for you, am I, my dear? Let me have one last try. Come back tomorrow and I promise I'll have the smiliest gingerbread men you have ever seen. Will you do that?"

"All right," said Anna-Maria. She wanted those gingerbread

men so very badly, but she couldn't bring herself to tell her aunty or the baker why.

The day had started badly for the baker, and it didn't improve when his regular customers started to complain about the bread he had allowed to rise for too long.

"It's just not up to your usual high standard," said the Mayor, brushing crumbs off his satin waistcoat. "What's the trouble? Anything I can help with?"

"No," cried the baker. "Just a silly problem last night. Nothing I can't deal with, I promise you. It won't happen again."

But that night, the baker was so tired that he could hardly tell *what* he was doing. The only thing he could think of was Anna-Maria's sad little face.

He finished his other baking as quickly as he could (and perhaps he didn't take quite as much care as usual), then cleared his table so that he could concentrate all his efforts on the gingerbread men. This time, they must be absolutely perfect.

Soon six little gingerbread men were sitting on a baking tray, ready to go into the oven. They had one smiley cherry mouth. They had two little currant eyes. They had three currant buttons in a row down their tummies. They were just right.

With a sigh of relief, the busy baker popped the little biscuits into the oven and sat down.

He was exhausted! Slowly, his eyelids began to droop. His head began to nod. In less than a minute, he fell fast asleep at his bakery table.

Meanwhile, in the oven, the gingerbread men turned a lovely golden brown. But the busy baker slept on. The gingerbread men began to look a little toasted around their toes. But the busy baker's eyes didn't open. The buttons on the gingerbread men's tummies began to sizzle, until they turned into little black cinders. But the busy baker didn't stir. Soon the smell of burnt gingerbread filled the bakery, and it was joined by the smell of burnt bread and burnt cakes and burnt biscuits. As the smell drifted across the bakery and tickled the baker's nose, he *jumped* out of his chair with a mighty shout.

"My bread!" he cried, flinging open the oven door. "My cakes! My biscuits! My gingerbread men!"

Everything looked dreadful. The busy baker couldn't imagine that even the ducks on the village pond would want to peck at his burnt offerings.

In despair, the baker glanced at the clock. It was almost seven o'clock in the morning. There was no time to make anything now.

The baker felt bad about his bread and cakes and biscuits. He knew how disappointed all his customers would be. But most of all, he felt awful about the little girl who was pinning her hopes on six smiley gingerbread men.

Anna-Maria wasn't waiting when the busy baker opened his shop door that morning, although several other villagers were. They stared in disbelief as the baker pinned up a notice. Within minutes, news of the bakery disaster was all over the village.

No Bread   No Cakes   No Biscuits

TODAY

Normal service resumes tomorrow.

No one felt angry with the baker. They all knew how hard he worked. They just felt very worried. What if he became really ill? And all because he always tried to do his best for his customers? Before the morning was over, the Mayor had called an Extraordinary Meeting, and everyone in the village (except the baker himself, who was sitting sadly in his empty shop) was trying to think of an idea that would help to make sure the poor man never became so tired again.

Things began to improve for the baker in the afternoon. And

what had started off as the worst
day of his life, soon became the
very best.

At two o'clock, a little face
peeped round the shop door.
The baker hardly recognised it,
because it had the sunniest smile
he had ever seen. It was Anna-
Maria, and holding her hand was
a lady smiling just as broadly.
The baker knew at once that it
must be the little girl's mother.
Their smiles were so alike.

"This is my mummy," said
Anna-Maria. "She is better now
and has come to take me home.
And she brought me a present. I
thought you might like one,

because I heard what happened last night."

The little girl held out a gingerbread man, made by her own dear mummy. It was rather wobbly looking, and its smile was crooked, but the baker could see that Anna-Maria thought it was the best gingerbread man in the world. And she was right.

Just then, a group of villagers arrived at the door.

"We've come to help," they said. "You need some assistants, and we are going to take turns. We can start at once."

"Hurray!" the baker mumbled ... with his mouth full!

The Giant
Boots

Twinkletown is usually a quiet place. Perhaps it's because it has such a silly name that not very much seems to happen there. The elves who live in Twinkletown generally go about their business without much fuss, and I can't remember the last time there was anything as dramatic as a fire or an outbreak of sneezles. (In case you don't know, that's an illness only elves suffer from. It makes them giggle and sneeze at the same time, and it's quite difficult to cure.)

So, with Twinkletown being such a quiet place, you can imagine how amazed everyone was when they woke up one morning to find a pair of giant boots standing on the poppleball pitch. (I'll explain poppleball another time.)

Of course, it would be pretty astonishing to find a pair of giant boots *anywhere* (except on a pair of giant feet), but to find them in Twinkletown really did seem most extraordinary.

Even before breakfast (and elves, as you know, love a big breakfast), several elves had gathered around the boots.

"I've never seen anything like it," said Mugwort, who was a very old elf and had seen most things in his time, although he couldn't always remember what he had seen yesterday.

"They must have arrived in the night," gasped Umpelty, who had a genius for stating the obvious.

"Well done, Einstein," said Twig, one of the cleverer elves in Twinkletown, which is not renowned for cleverness. "They look to me," he went on, "like *giant* boots."

"Well, of course they're giant boots," said Mugwort testily. "No one in his right mind would call them *tiny* boots."

"No," sighed Twig, "that's not what I mean. I mean they look

like the kind of boots that might belong to a *giant*."

A very long silence greeted these words. Everyone was disturbed by the idea of a giant. Suddenly, all minds were filled with questions.

""Where's the giant?" asked Mugwort, looking anxious.

"Are giants friendly?" asked Umpelty, looking worried.

"And more to the point, wherever he is, and however friendly he is, *why isn't he wearing his boots*?" asked Twig.

Slowly, all three elves spun round on their heels, as if they expected to see that a bootless giant had been sneaking up behind them in his socks. But everything looked exactly as usual – except for the boots.

"We shall have to have a meeting," said Umpelty, who found it very hard to make a decision without other people telling him what to think.

"We certainly shall," said Mugwort, who welcomed any opportunity to listen to the sound of his own voice.

"I suppose so," said Twig, who knew that an elfin meeting could go on for days without coming to any very great conclusion – much like human meetings, in fact.

We have a few moments, while the elves are getting together for their meeting and arguing about which seats to sit in, so I'll tell you about poppleball. It's a very silly game indeed, which only elves would want to play (with the possible exception of fairies, who are, if anything, sillier than elves). You have to balance a ball on the end of your nose and run backwards towards the goal, which is shaped like a laundry basket and has, for no very good reason that I've ever been able to discover, bananas painted all over it. The idea is not, as you might expect, to throw the ball into the goal, but to jump into it yourself, without dropping the ball from your nose. Unless you are cheating in the worst possible way (and most elves wouldn't dream of cheating), it is almost impossible to score. Games of poppleball invariably end with a score of 0–0, with the result that the league table is one of the most predictable items ever printed in the Elf Gazette.

Right, now the elves are settled in their seats, so we must go back to the meeting.

The first person to speak was the only elf who had ever actually met a giant. His name was Diggle, and he had once travelled a great deal.

"The giant that I met," he said, "was a really nasty piece of work. He hated anyone smaller than himself and often made them into pies. Perhaps some giants are nicer. I don't know. But what I find very strange about this whole business is that the giant I knew would never have dreamed of taking off his boots. He wore them in bed and when he took a bath (which was not very often). Why has *our* giant taken his boots *off*?"

Unfortunately, Diggle had to repeat most of his speech

because almost everyone stopped listening in horror when he got to the bit about little-person-pies.

When the whole speech had finally been understood, an elf at the back of the room waved a heavy book in the air.

"I've got a dictionary here," called Parsley. "It confirms just what you say. Listen:

'**Giant** *n.* A very large person with unpleasant eating habits. Wears seven-league boots, which he never removes.'

It sounds as though Diggle is right about the abandoned boots. Where *is* the giant?"

"Just a minute," put in Twig, "*are* those seven-league boots? They don't look much bigger than four-and-a-half-league boots to me." (And that just goes to show that Twig can sometimes talk just as much nonsense as the next elf, because I happen to know that he doesn't have the faintest idea how far a league is.)

I won't bore you with the next forty-two hours of the meeting. At the end of them, nothing very much had been decided and just as much silliness was being spouted as at the beginning. It was when Twig was trying to raise his four-and-a-half-league

question for the nineteenth time
that a small voice shouted out
from the back of the hall.

"Excuse me! I say, excuse me!"

No one paid any attention at
all. An argument had broken out
about whether seven leagues
was longer than forty-three
furlongs, as if that had anything
at all to do with the subject on
hand – or on foot – or, actually,
not on foot!

"Excuse me!" The voice came
again. "Could someone come and
help me with my boots?"

Again, no one paid any
attention, but five minutes later,
when there was a lull in the

conversation, Mugwort suddenly asked, "Did someone mention boots?" And just as everyone was about to raise their eyebrows at the old man's foolishness, because, after all, they had been talking about boots for the past two days, the little voice at the back shouted again, more loudly.

"Yes!" it said. "I left some boots on your field last night and I wondered if half a dozen of you strong young elves could help me move them."

All eyes turned on the stranger, who turned out to be an ordinary looking elf with quite small feet.

To cut a long story short, the elf was a bootmaker. For the purposes of advertising his work, he had made a pair of giant boots, which he took around with him on a truck. The night before, the truck had broken down, and rather than trying to tow it with the boots on board, the elf had decided to leave them in the field, confident that the local elves would be talking about what to do well into the middle of the week.

"The only trouble is," said the bootmaker elf, "that the truck is getting old and really can't carry more than one boot any more. I don't really *need* two, so I was wondering if I could leave one of them here with you."

"I'll look after it," called an old woman who had so many children she didn't know what to do, but that is another story, and you probably know it already.

So it was that the most exciting thing to happen in Twinkletown for years turned out to be about as exciting as … well … as the score at the end of a game of poppleball!

Where's
That
Sheep?

If he had said it once, he had said it a hundred times. Poor Farmer Forrest was in despair. At any time of the day you might see him look up from his work towards the top meadow and cry in exasperation, "Now where's that sheep?"

Yes, Molly was a sheep who loved to wander. She wasn't a stay-at-home-and-wait-for-your-wool-to-grow kind of sheep at all. At the sight of a lowish wall, a thinnish hedge or a weakish fence, Molly was off. She didn't run or make a noise or draw attention to herself in any way. She simply trotted off down the

lane. It was sometimes hours before anyone noticed she was gone at all.

But after her fourth escape attempt, Farmer Forrest became wise to Molly's ways. He put her in the top meadow, where he could keep an eye on her. Whenever he lifted his eyes from his work, he checked to see that she was there. But still the cry was heard at least once a week. "Now where's that sheep?"

To be fair, it wasn't really Molly's fault. You see, Farmer Forrest didn't keep sheep as a rule. He had cows, pigs and a few hens, but he had never farmed

sheep. It was only when Mrs
Forrest took up spinning that she
begged her husband to invest in
a flock.

"But I don't know anything
about sheep!" complained her
husband. "Besides, this isn't the
right kind of country for them.
No one for miles around has
sheep. Can't you just buy a
fleece to spin?"

But Mrs Forrest argued that it
just wouldn't be the same. To
spin wool from a sheep that had
lived on your own land, that
would be really satisfying.

"And I can just see you
wearing the jumper I would knit,"

she told her husband. Think how proud you would be."

"All right," said Farmer Forrest, "but not a whole flock. We'll start with one sheep and see how we get on. That's only sensible."

Mrs Forrest reluctantly agreed, but in fact this was very far from sensible. You see, sheep are sociable animals. They like to be with a whole group of their own kind. They're not loners at heart. That was why Molly set off to find some like-minded sheep at every opportunity. As I said, it really wasn't her fault.

But Farmer Forrest found that he was wasting an enormous

amount of time running around the countryside looking for that sheep. She nearly always trotted off in the same direction, as she had a strong feeling that there were other sheep to the north of her, but even so, there were many winding lanes around Forrest Farm, and it sometimes took the farmer the best part of a morning to find her.

"You know," Farmer Forrest said to his wife, "this can't go on. You'll have to find somewhere else to supply you with wool. I can't keep spending time running after that sheep. I'm far too busy at this time of year."

"Oh, but if you could just wait another couple of weeks, pleaded Mrs Forrest, "it would be time to shear her. Once I've got my fleece, you can sell her if you like, although I must confess that I've become rather fond of Molly. She's got such an independent spirit."

"Independent spirit my big toe!" scoffed her husband. As

soon as she's shorn, that sheep can go and be independent somewhere else."

A couple of days before the shearing, as Mr and Mrs Forrest were sitting at breakfast, Mrs Forrest raised the subject again.

"Honeybun," she began.

"Don't call me that," growled Mr Forrest.

"How would you like a whole flock of sheep like Molly?"

"We've been through this before," said Mr Forrest. "I've told you, I am not a sheep farmer."

"Well," said his wife, pointing with her cereal spoon, "I think you are now."

Mr Forrest followed her gaze. Up in the top meadow was a flock of sheep. Not one lonely Molly but at least fifteen sheep.

"What on earth…?" Mr Forrest hurried from his chair and threw on his coat. This had to be sorted out.

But when he drew near the meadow, he found that his eyes had not been playing tricks on him. There really were fifteen sheep grazing happily on the juicy grass. And only one of them was Molly. To be honest, despite his many trips across the countryside to bring her home, Mr Forrest wouldn't have been quite sure which sheep *was* Molly, but Mrs Forrest had followed him from the farmhouse, and she at once pointed out their own sheep.

"But where have these others come from?" asked Mr Forrest. "None of them have markings or collars or tags as far as I can see."

"I haven't the faintest idea," said his wife. "We'll have to think how we can find out who owns them. They do look *lovely* up here though, don't they?"

Mr Forrest grunted and went off to his work, while Mrs Forrest hurried back to the farmhouse.

The telephone was ringing as she arrived.

"Oh, Deidre," said a voice. "Thank goodness I've caught you. Something dreadful has happened. We've lost Hortense."

Mrs Forrest recognised the voice of one of the members of her spinning circle.

"Hortense?" she queried. "Is that your daughter?"

"No, no, no," cried the caller. "It's my sheep. The one I was going to have sheared next week. How am I going to find her?"

"Well, you could ask my husband," suggested Mrs Forrest. "He's had quite a lot of experience of finding sheep, especially just lately."

But even as she was speaking, Mrs Forrest was getting the funny feeling that she had seen Hortense rather more recently than her friend had.

"Let me call you back," said Mrs Forrest. "I just need to check something out."

Over the next few minutes, Mrs Forrest telephoned six of her spinning-circle friends. Every one of them reported a sheep that had gone missing during the past night. The farmer's wife felt pretty sure that other members would report a similar event.

"Oh, *clever* Molly," breathed Mrs Forrest. She realised now that the sheep must have made several friends in a similar situation as she roamed the countryside on her many bids for escape.

The sheep were so happy all together in the meadow that no one had the heart to send them all home – even Farmer Forrest. So Mrs Forrest became the official shepherdess of the spinning circle.

I wouldn't like to promise that Molly has wandered off for the last time, though. I did hear that there was a solitary sheep over in Farmbridge. And if I heard it, I expect Molly did too...

The Mouse's House

Now there are those who enjoy keeping their things clean and tidy and there are those who don't. You can tell as soon as you step inside someone's front door which kind of home you are visiting. Of course, it is nice not to have to move piles of books and papers before you sit in a chair. And no one wants to find their plate covered in a thick layer of dust, but some people are *so* clean and tidy that it's no fun at all to pay them a visit. The Mouse was like that, as you will see.

The Mouse lived in a very cosy little tree-trunk house in the

middle of Mendlesham Wood. She probably had been given a proper name when she was a baby, but everyone just called her "Mouse".

Mouse had always been proud of her home, and she had never been untidy. She liked everything to look just right, so that none of the other animals in Mendlesham wood could point their paws at her and say, "Have you *seen* the cobwebs in *her* house?"

But to begin with, Mouse was no more worried about dirt and dust than any moderately houseproud animal in the wood. The change was very gradual.

For a long time, she swept her front steps once a day. Then you might sometimes see her, especially in autumn, giving them a little extra sweep in the afternoon. By the time of this story, she was out on those steps half a dozen times a day.

"It's these horrible old leaves," she would say, if a friend protested that she was working too hard.

"But Mouse, you live in a *tree*!" the friend would say. "Of course there will be leaves."

"Not on my steps there won't!" replied Mouse stoutly, picking up her broom again.

Well, Mouse became as particular about the inside of her house as she was about her front steps. She was constantly dusting and sweeping and washing and wiping. She was a great plumper-up of cushions, too, and she had a hatred of spiders and their webs that would have been funny if it hadn't been rather worrying too.

"Out of my way," Mouse would say to a guest who had come to tea. "I saw one of those pesky little animals run under your chair. I can't rest until I've found him. The very thought of those eight muddy feet running over my floorboards makes me shiver and shake. Watch out! Don't spill your tea!"

It soon became something of a lottery to visit Mouse. You might have a perfectly lovely time, but on her worst days, Mouse was not a good hostess.

"Excuse me, but *did* you wipe your feet as you came in?" she would ask, peering suspiciously at your shoes. "Perhaps you wouldn't mind doing it again."

Then, after you had dutifully wiped them up and down several times on the doormat, Mouse would make a big point of shaking the mat itself outside the door. Of course, that might mean that she felt the step needed sweeping as well. So you see what I mean, conversation at Mouse's tea parties was often a little strained.

Gradually, the animals in Mendlesham Wood became quite worried about Mouse.

"It isn't healthy to be so finicky," said the owl, whose own home was really none too clean. "Mouse is making herself ill worrying about things that don't matter at all. Why, when I visited her the other day, she told me I couldn't sit in the chairs because I'd flatten the cushions. I mean,

what are chairs *for*? That's what I'd like to know."

"It was the same when I called to collect her grocery money," said the rabbit who lived under the old oak tree. "She wouldn't let me knock at the front door in case my paws were dirty. She was peering out of the window, waiting for me, so that she could catch me before I touched it!"

"That's dreadful," said the hedgehog. "Doesn't she know that a little bit of dirt is *good* for you. That's what I always tell my little ones."

Some of the others coughed and looked away. They knew very well that the hedgehog and her little ones were never invited to Mouse's house because it was well known by everyone that they had *fleas*. Mouse hated fleas almost as much as she hated spiders. Just because they hopped instead of scurrying, it didn't mean that their feet were clean. Very few tiny creatures were welcome in Mouse's home, although she did have a soft spot for moths, for some reason.

"Someone should talk to her," said the owl. "A close friend, I mean," he went on hurriedly, "not someone like me who is really only an acquaintance."

"The sad thing is that she really doesn't *have* any close friends any more," said the squirrel. "It is so uncomfortable to visit her now that nobody wants to do it. And it's hard to be close friends with an animal you hardly ever see. I can't remember the last time I visited Mouse's house, in fact. I miss having her as a friend."

"I think you're right," said the woodpecker. "I haven't seen her since I made that little attic window at the back for her a few years ago. She complained about the sawdust then, but she was nothing like so fussy as she is now. I don't think she could bear anyone to touch her house in any way."

The animals were well meaning, but they couldn't really think of any way to help Mouse. In the end, it was a complete stranger who made a difference.

That winter was particularly cold. Even the trees shuddered as a howling, icy wind whistled

around their roots and branches,
frosting their twigs and chilling
every little creature who lived
nearby. All the animals huddled
in their homes, doing the best
they could to keep warm.

Mouse had a snugger home
than most, especially as she
always made sure that her
window frames were free from
draughts and her strong, tree-
trunk walls were free from cracks.

But Mouse didn't like the way
that frost made her windows
look dirty, and snow had a habit
of dropping from the branches
above and falling with an
alarming *plop!* on to her steps.

It was on a particularly cold and blustery night that Mouse had an unexpected visitor. She was sitting in front of her fire, sipping a cup of apple tea, when she heard a little squeal outside and then a hammering at her door. Mouse tried to ignore it at first, but then the dreadful thought occurred to her that someone might actually be damaging her home. She pulled her shawl around her shoulders and opened the door.

Outside was a truly pitiful sight. A little mouse, no bigger than Mouse herself, was shivering on the doorstep.

"Please," he said, "could I come in to warm myself for a moment? I won't trouble you for long."

Mouse hesitated for just a second. She thought with horror of the mouse's wet little paws scampering across her sitting room. She shuddered at the thought of his cold, wet little body sitting on one of her chairs. She could imagine the way that he would shake his whiskers all over her carefully polished table. But Mouse could not bear to see another creature suffer, so she stood back from the door.

"Do come in," she said. "Er … the door mat is just here."

"Thank you so much," shivered the stranger mouse, as he stood in the middle of Mouse's sitting room. "I don't think I could have lasted much longer out there. It's no night for a mouse to be out."

"No, indeed," agreed Mouse. "Er … can I take your … er … coat?" She didn't really think that was the right word for the ragged, shapeless garment that the mouse held tightly around himself. But the mouse seemed to know what she meant and handed her the thin, wet cloth.

"I've been travelling for a long time," he said. "I'm on my way to see someone very special, but winter has been harder than I ever thought it would be. I should probably have put off my journey until the spring, but I was so eager to meet this person that I couldn't wait."

Mouse handed the stranger a towel to dry his whiskers before he shook them any more, but the visitor didn't seem to understand and wrapped the towel around his shoulders instead.

"Thank you again," he said. "I should introduce myself. My name is George."

The name sounded vaguely familiar to Mouse, but she couldn't think why.

"My name is Mouse," she said. "It sounds strange, I know, but I think it's what I've always been called. I can't remember when I was a baby."

George nodded and sat down in the chair. Thankfully the towel was between him and the upholstery. Goodness knew when he had last taken a bath.

The newcomer was still shivering, so Mouse hurried to her neat little kitchen and made up a tray of hot soup, bread and juniper biscuits.

"I wasn't expecting visitors," she said, apologising for the makeshift supper. And all of a sudden she wondered why that was. There had been a time when her friends visited her every day, but she couldn't remember now the last time that anyone had dropped in.

George didn't find the supper disappointing at all. He was already finishing the soup and stuffing a rather large piece of bread into his mouth.

"This is wonderful," he said, between chews. "I haven't had anything to eat since the day before yesterday."

Mouse was horrified to hear this. In fact, she was so concerned that she didn't notice until it was too late that George had put his hot soup bowl down on her polished table. She snatched it up with a cry. Sure enough, there was a white ring where the bowl had stood.

"Ooops, sorry," said George.

Mouse knew that she could not possibly send her visitor out into the blizzard again tonight. She hurried upstairs and made sure that the sheets on the spare-room bed were aired. She slipped a hot water bottle into the bed and ran back downstairs again to try to stop George doing any more damage to her furniture. She was too late.

"I am ever so sorry," said George. "I don't know how it happened. One minute I was rocking myself gently in your chair and the next minute the leg fell off. It must have been a little loose, I think."

"Rocking?" said Mouse faintly. She looked up at the wall, and sure enough she could see the mark where the chair had been bumped over and over again. This mouse would bring her home down about her ears if he carried on at this rate!

Nevertheless, Mouse clenched her paws and asked George if he would like a bath before bed.

"That would be bliss," said George. "I haven't had a bath since…"

"Yes, yes, that's all right," said Mouse hurriedly. She really didn't feel she could cope with the news George had been about to give her.

Five minutes later, Mouse, doing her best to tidy up downstairs, heard George singing at the top of his voice. It was a very silly song, and he wasn't remotely in tune, but still she caught herself smiling. It was such a long time since she had heard anyone really enjoying themselves in her house.

But Mouse's smile was not in place for long. She began to wonder what state the bathroom would be in when George had finished, and just then … *splosh!* … a drop of water bounced off her nose.

Mouse looked up in horror. There was no doubt about it, water was dripping through her beautiful ceiling and on to her sofa below.

Mouse hurried up the stairs and banged furiously on the bathroom door.

"W-w-w-what?" came a voice, after a moment. "Oh no! Oh, I am sorry. I dozed off for a moment and left the taps running. There's not much water on the floor though. Honestly, there isn't."

"That's because it's on the floor downstairs," muttered Mouse to herself, but she felt sorry for the little mouse who was so tired he had almost drowned himself.

A moment later, George appeared at the bathroom door, wearing a pair of Mouse's late father's pyjamas. He looked clean and scrubbed, but his eyelids were drooping, and he had one paw on the door frame to support himself as he said goodnight to his hostess.

"Goodnight," said Mouse. "I hope you sleep well."

It took Mouse another three hours to finish clearing up the sitting room *and* the bathroom, but then her standards were very high. She was exhausted herself when she finally tottered up the stairs to bed. And that is why she fell asleep the moment her head touched the pillow and didn't wake up at the crack of dawn as usual in the morning.

In fact, Mouse woke up feeling rather happy with the world. It took a few seconds for her to realise that this was because the smell of a fried breakfast and freshly brewed acorn coffee was wafting up the stairs.

Mouse sat up in bed. Someone was in her kitchen! Then the events of the night before came flooding back. Oh no! *George* was in her kitchen, and what was more, he was *cooking*!

Mouse flew out of bed and into her dressing gown. Her little feet hardly touched the stairs as she rushed towards the kitchen. One glimpse was enough to tell her that it was even worse than she had feared. There was George, his whiskers singed, flapping a tea towel at a flaming pan, while water running into the sink overflowed on to the floor. A second glimpse showed her two broken cups and a fish slice bent in two. And surely that wasn't … oh no, it couldn't be … that wasn't a *pancake* stuck to the ceiling? Mouse had to sit down in a hurry, and the floor was the nearest place.

"Oh, there you are," called George cheerfully. "I was just making you a little breakfast to thank you for being so kind. If you just wait there while I deal with this little fire, it will be ready for you in just a minute."

Mouse put her head in her hands. George was going to have

to go, and he was going to have to go *soon*. She felt that every second that George spent in her house was another opportunity for disaster to strike.

But just at that moment, the visitor pushed a plate of pancakes and syrup under her nose. Much to Mouse's surprise, it smelt *delicious*! With all the excitement the night before, she remembered, she hadn't had any supper herself. Now she was too hungry to do anything other than pick up a spoon and start eating. And the pancakes tasted as delicious as they looked. How extraordinary!

As she munched her way through the pancakes, Mouse became aware that her visitor was talking.

"… so that's why I felt I just had to come and see her," he was saying. "I've heard so many stories about how kind she is to everyone, and how animals flock to see her when they are in trouble. Aunt Petunia sounds such a wonderful person. I don't suppose you know her, do you? She lives somewhere around here. In fact, I'm sure you two must be friends, for you are just as kind as she is. *Do* you know her, Mouse?"

Mouse had the strangest feeling in her tail and whiskers. Petunia! That was a name she hadn't heard for so long. For the first time in years, Mouse knew what her real name was. No wonder George had looked and sounded familiar. He was her own sister Salvia's son.

If Mouse hadn't been sitting down already, she would have done so now. Instead, she asked George if she could have some of his acorn coffee.

Huddled in her dressing gown, Mouse sipped the excellent coffee and thought hard. There *had* been a time when she cared

more for others than for herself.
What had happened? Mouse
looked around her home. In
recent years, she had cared more
for cleaning and tidying than for
anything that was really
important. Mouse felt ashamed.
How could she confess who she
was to this eager young mouse,
when the evidence was all too
plain that she only ever thought
about her perfect home.

Then Mouse began to laugh.
The evidence wasn't plain at all!
Her kitchen was in ruins. The
sitting room ceiling was soggy.
There were marks on the walls
and furniture, and she hadn't

even looked to see what George had done to the spare room.

Mouse looked again at her nephew. He was certainly a wonderful cook. He just needed a little guidance about safety and damage control. Mouse felt warmed by the idea that George might have to stay for a few weeks, months or even years, so that she could help him.

For the first time in ages, Mouse felt really happy, and that made her laugh too, especially as the flood on the floor was now creeping up her dressing gown.

"George," she smiled, "there's quite a lot I need to tell you..."

The
Travelling
Tree

Once upon a time, there was a very fine tree who lived in a forest. He was perfectly happy there, surrounded by his friends. He imagined that one day the whole forest would be cut down for timber. Then he would be carted off to a new life, and he would be able to see a little bit more of the world.

But when the time came for the forest to be felled, a very strange thing happened. All the trees around our tree were cut down, but he was left. Now, instead of standing in the middle of a forest, he stood on a huge area of open ground.

The tree could not think why he, of all the forest, had been left, and to tell you the truth, neither can I, but that is what happened. At first, the tree tried to make the best of it. It was nice to be able to look at the countryside, instead of seeing nothing but other trees. But the novelty of his situation soon wore off. The tree was bored and lonely. The land around stretched, flat and barren, for miles. After being covered with trees for so long, it was not yet able to grow other plants. There were not even any flowers. The tree felt increasingly unhappy.

But what can a tree do to improve his situation? He can't hurry off to complain to the authorities or find a more interesting place to live. Or can he?

The more the tree thought about it, the more convinced he became that he could move, if he only put his mind to it. Yes, I know, trees don't move. Well, they wave their branches in the wind, but they don't suddenly stroll off down the street, do they? However, our tree was determined. When he made up his mind that he wanted to move, that was it. He put all his energy into doing just that.

One fine spring morning, when anything seemed possible, the tree decided to try to move. He stood up very straight and concentrated as hard as he could on his roots. He thought and thought and thought, and suddenly, just when he was beginning to give up hope, one of his roots gave a distinct wiggle.

The tree tried again. This time, another root gave a little twitch. This was going to be a much slower process than he had imagined. The tree realised that he was likely to have to spend quite some time doing warming-up exercises before he was ready to wander off across the open plain. But he had made a start. That was the important thing.

Over the next few weeks, the tree practised hard every day. Pretty soon, he could wiggle his roots with hardly a thought. In fact, by wiggling them all at once, he could make himself jiggle about a little on the spot. He wasn't exactly moving, but he wasn't exactly standing still, either. The tree began to feel more cheerful.

It was after several days of wiggling and jiggling that the tree thought he might be ready to try something more ambitious. He dug his front roots into the ground, lifted his back roots as high as he could, and tried to sway forward. The tree had seen people walking, and he was pretty sure he wouldn't be able to manage that. After all, people have two legs, and they sort of sway from one to the other. Trees either have lots of legs (their roots) or one leg (their trunk), depending on which way you think about it.

The tree had decided that the best way to walk would be to rock backwards and forwards, using his roots to alternately push and pull himself over the ground. His first attempt was not very successful, but it did confirm his idea that this was the way to go. He practised harder than ever over the next few weeks.

By the time the tree felt he was really ready to try to move a few paces, it was nearly autumn. The tree was desperate to begin his journey before the winter's ice made it hard to get a grip on the ground. He told himself that he would take his first steps the next day, as soon as it was light, and settled down to have a good night's sleep, so that he would be fresh in the morning.

The morning dawned bright and breezy. The tree stretched up as tall as he could, braced his trunk, and wobbled forward.

He didn't topple over. He didn't twizzle round. No, he moved about six inches. He was on his way!

Now trees, even very athletic ones, do not move very quickly. Our tree inched his way across the plain incredibly slowly. But it was still quick enough to make a passing rabbit more surprised than he had ever been in his life. And anyone nearby would have been able to see a kind of furrow left behind the tree as he moved.

If you add together enough inches, you make a mile. And if you add together enough miles, you can go anywhere in the world you like. So it was that the tree inched its way over a small rise one day and saw a little town in the distance.

A winding road led to the town, but the tree didn't think he would be any good at walking on a road, so he set off across the fields. Even though the tree moved incredibly slowly, it still caused puzzlement to one or two local people, who were pretty sure they hadn't ever seen a tree in the fields next to the road. But what are you going to say to your friends about that? "Oh, I saw a tree where there's never been a tree before today. Isn't that strange?" I'm afraid it's you that would be thought strange.

Well, day after day, the tree crept closer and closer to the

town, until he was towering over the first little cottage.

Unfortunately, the tree had never seen a cottage before. He didn't know that the people inside need to get in and out, or that it is the door that lets them do this. So the tree stood beside the cottage, right in front of the only door.

In the morning, the father of the family got ready to go to work as usual. He put on his coat and opened the door. *Clunk!* The door opened about two inches before it hit the tree. The man couldn't see anything through the crack in the door, so he

peered through the letterbox.
Then he ran up to the attic to
look out of the little window
there to check that he was not
going completely mad. No, there
was a tree standing in front of
the door.

The man had a vague feeling
that he'd seen just such a tree at
the bottom of the garden a few
weeks back. But what was it
doing now blocking his door?

Always a resourceful fellow,
the man rigged up some flags
from the attic window, to attract
the attention of passing
townsfolk so that they would
come to the rescue.

Sure enough, it was not long before quite a group of people had gathered in front of the cottage. As is often the case with such groups, they were much more interested in talking about *what* had happened and *why* than they were in rescuing the poor man and his family inside.

"But how did it *get* here?" the trapped family heard someone say more than once.

"Never mind how it got here!" bellowed the man through the letterbox. "Just get us out!"

All day the discussion went on, with the family inside getting more and more aggrieved. At last the leader of the group, who also happened to be the Mayor, leaned round the tree and banged on the only part of the door he could reach.

"I say! Are you in there?" he called loudly.

I'm afraid that the reply of the cottage's owner is not in the least printable, which is not surprising really.

"We've decided what we need to do!" called the Mayor.

"Thank goodness for that!" yelled the man inside. "What?"

"What?"

"I said, what are you going to do? How long will it take?"

"Oh, we'll have to come back tomorrow," called the Mayor. "It is much too late to start now. We've decided we're going to cut the tree down."

"It's taken you all day to decide *that*?" yelled the man inside. And there was another unprintable bit.

The Mayor looked up. Was it his imagination, or did the tree give a kind of a shudder?

"It's a very fine tree," he called. "The kind that anyone would be glad to have in their garden."

"But not in front of their door!" The man inside was exasperated beyond belief, but he could see that there was no chance of persuading the Mayor to do anything sensible tonight.

"Oh, never mind!" he called. "But I'll be expecting you first thing in the morning!"

Even as the townsfolk were slowly walking home, still wondering about the amazing tree, the tree itself was thinking hard. Although, in the past, he had been quite happy at the thought of being cut down, now it didn't seem such an attractive idea. He would never be able to walk across the countryside again! That was no fate for a travelling tree.

The tree waited until it was dark, then it stretched up tall and used every ounce of its energy to hurl itself away from the cottage. The tree had become very strong during its journey, and it had not moved at all during the day, so now it was feeling fresh and vigorous. You would have been astonished to see the speed with which the tree swayed across the garden and into the neighbouring field. Of course, the townsfolk would have been even more astonished, for they were still thinking that the tree had been moved by witchcraft or a freak storm.

But the tree had learned its lesson. Letting humans see what it was doing was going to be more trouble than it was worth. You never knew when they were going to have their axes with them, and although the tree could move very quickly for a *tree*, it could never outpace a human being.

The tree knew it would have to hide. If it could hide by day, then at night it could travel to its heart's content. *Hide?* I know what you are thinking. How on earth can you hide an enormous tree? You can't just throw a sheet over it and pretend it isn't there.

But the tree had learnt a lot on his travels, and now he did something very clever indeed. He got behind a thick hedge and *lay down*! Yes, his roots and his trunk had become so supple, he just lay down, out of sight.

So next morning, the tree-chopping party led by the Mayor was a comical sight. And the next night, the tree made good his escape.

I believe he is still on the move somewhere, and you may well have seen him. Keep an eye on the trees in your neighbourhood, and if you see a visiting one, say hello from me!

Are You Ready, Eddy?

Once upon a time, there was a group of boys who played in a band. They practised very hard and soon became so good that they were always invited to perform at the village fête in the summer and for the carol-singers in the winter. And very often, during the year, they would be asked to play a few tunes at a party, or a wedding, or a ceremony at the village hall.

Everyone was happy. The boys made lots of pocket money (which was just as well, because instruments are very expensive), and the village had its own little band it could call on.

There was only one problem, and that was Eddy. Now Eddy played the trumpet like an angel. *That* wasn't the problem. He could sing beautifully too, and sometimes did a chorus of *Silent Night* when the band trotted round the village with the carol-singers. In almost every way, Eddy was a perfect member of the band, if only he wasn't always late!

It didn't matter how carefully the boys discussed their arrangements beforehand, when they called at Eddy's house on the edge of the village, it was always the same.

"Are you ready, Eddy?" they would shout.

"Nearly," Eddy would call back, and the other boys would groan, because they knew what "nearly" meant. It didn't mean, "I've just got to put my socks on and I'll be with you." It didn't mean, "I'm running down the stairs right now." It didn't even mean, "Just let me comb my hair and clean my shoes and I'll be there." It meant, "Sometime in the next hour or so, I might be ready to join you."

As you can imagine, it drove the other boys absolutely wild. They had tried everything to solve the problem. Bobby had been appointed Eddy's "minder", responsible for making sure he was ready, but after two weeks, Bobby resigned. He couldn't bear the mess in Eddy's bedroom, and he couldn't bear the vague way in which Eddy did everything at home. When they were playing, it was quite different. Eddy always came in at the right places and had his wits about him. At home, he was a different boy.

"I know just how you feel, Bobby," said Eddy's mother, when she found Bobby sitting in despair at the bottom of the stairs, waiting for her son.

"I don't know what to do about him. He just doesn't seem to have any idea of time," she went on. "Getting him to school in the morning is a nightmare. We'll make superhuman efforts to have his clothes and shoes ready. I'll stand over him until he's brushed his teeth and combed his hair. Then I'll just leave him to put his tie and shoes on. You wouldn't believe that a boy could take an hour to do something as simple as that."

"I would," groaned Bobby. "Oh, I would."

This state of affairs went on for so long that everyone had

become used to it. The boys in the band took to calling for Eddy at least two hours before he was needed. By hanging around outside and shouting up to his window every ten minutes, "Are you ready, Eddy?" they would eventually manage to get him out of the house.

Eddy's mother grew used to getting up a couple of hours early to get her son off to school. It was ridiculous, but no one could see another way to do it.

Then Eddy's Uncle Albert came to stay. He wasn't a real uncle, in fact. He had gone to school with Eddy's father and had long been a friend of the family. Eddy had called him Uncle Albert since he was tiny.

Now Uncle Albert had not visited for several years, as he had been working abroad, so he did not know about Eddy's lateness. He was shocked the first morning of his visit to find his hostess downstairs at the crack of dawn.

Eddy's mother explained the whole problem.

The next day was a Saturday, so Uncle Albert looked forward to being able to sleep in without being disturbed, but once again he was woken horribly early. He came muttering out of his room to find Bobby waiting patiently on the stairs. There was a wedding at nine o'clock, and Bobby was making quite sure that Eddy wouldn't be late, as he was playing a solo.

Uncle Albert sat down on the stairs with Bobby and listened to the whole story.

"But this is ridiculous!" he said. "Haven't you tried to stop it? You can't let it go on."

So Bobby told Uncle Albert about all the efforts that had been made to improve Eddy's timekeeping. He explained that Eddy had been talked to, pleaded with, shouted at, encouraged and even rewarded, but that nothing had worked.

"I see," said Uncle Albert. "Have you tried doing nothing?"

"Well," said Bobby, "that's what we're doing now, really."

"No, no," said Uncle Albert. "I mean nothing as in *not* arriving early for him."

"But he'll be late," said Bobby.

"Yes," said Uncle Albert. "But at least then he'll realise the consequences of his actions. He's not a bad lad, but I don't think at the moment he has any idea how much trouble people go to for him."

"You're probably right," said Bobby. "But we can't start today. The wedding…"

"Yes, yes, I understand," said Uncle Albert. "But we will start on Monday. Agreed?"

Bobby told the band about the new plan, and Uncle Albert told Eddy's mother.

The boys in the band agreed that it was worth a try.

"After all," said Bobby, "nothing else has worked."

Eddy's mother looked doubtful, but she was at her wits' end.

"Frankly, Albert," she said. "I'm willing to try anything. I'll leave it in your hands."

On Monday morning, no one shouted at Eddy to get ready for school. So he was late. By the time he finally wandered into the schoolyard, it was already time for morning break. His teacher told him not to let it happen again and gave him extra work.

On Monday evening, Eddy was so late for band practice that the other boys had gone home before he arrived. Eddy felt a little annoyed at this. They could have waited just a few minutes, couldn't they?

On Tuesday morning, Eddy was late for school again. This time the teacher was not so understanding. He gave Eddy extra homework and a lecture about punctuality.

On Tuesday evening, the band was supposed to be playing "Happy Birthday" to Mrs Marlow, who had celebrated her hundredth birthday that day. Luckily it was a tune that sounded all right without the trumpet, because Eddy failed to turn up at all.

On Wednesday morning, Eddy made an effort to get to school on time. It wasn't a very successful effort, because he was still twenty minutes late for his first class, but it was a start.

That evening, Eddy arrived at band practice about five minutes before it ended. Things were slowly improving.

It took three weeks, and a really quite unpleasant session with the headmaster, before Eddy began to arrive at school on time. With no one to shout at him, being punctual for band practice took a little longer, but it happened in the end.

Now, it has become a tradition that the band stands in front of their trumpeter's house and calls, "Are you ready, Eddy?" But there is never any reply, for Eddy is down in the street shouting too!

The
House
That Grew

Many years ago, there lived a goblin who was lazy. Goblins are usually very vigorous, hardworking people, but this one, whose name was Boxwood, was really not very energetic. If there was an easy way to do something, he always took it. If there was a corner to be cut, he cut it. And that is perhaps why Boxwood always looked as if he had been pulled through a hedge backwards. He never could be bothered to sew on a button, so his clothes were held together with safety pins.

Things improved a great deal for Boxwood when he married a

very sensible goblin called Dahlia. She soon smartened Boxwood up and made his home, which had not really been the kind of place you would want to visit, into a little palace.

Pretty soon, Dahlia's and Boxwood's first baby arrived. It was a little boy, and you have never seen a prouder father than Boxwood. A couple of years later, a little girl was born. Boxwood was beside himself with joy. But when Dahlia had twins the following year, Boxwood's delight was tinged with anxiety. It was all right now, when the children were still quite tiny, but where would they sleep when they were older?

Now, a sensible goblin would have done as Dahlia suggested and built an extension on to the back of the house. But Boxwood still had moments when he was not a very sensible goblin. He felt sure that there must be an easier way to make home improvements.

A few days later, Boxwood had the glimmering of an idea. He hurried down to the Lending Library to see if he could find some more information. But he was disappointed. There were lots of books on do-it-yourself but none mentioned what Boxwood

had in mind. He knew that he would have to go to an expert.

Old Millet lived by the stream that wound through the goblin town. He was a wise old goblin, with a friendly face. He was said to be wiser and cleverer than any goblin before him. And what was more, he was one of the few goblins who still remembered how to do magic.

There was a time when goblins used magic a great deal, but magic is dangerous stuff in the wrong hands. After some quite awful disasters, it was decided by the Goblin Council that only one goblin in each town or village would be allowed to practise magic, and that would be the wisest, most sensible goblin found to be living there.

Gradually, however, the use of magic almost died out. That was because wise, sensible goblins draw the line at using magic to do homework, brew up a love potion, or paint another goblin's house purple for a joke.

Somehow, the fun had gone out of magic, and it was very little used.

Boxwood arrived at Millet's house early one morning. He was polite and well dressed, so Millet, who didn't get out much any more, didn't realise quite what a silly goblin Boxwood was.

When Millet's visitor explained that he wanted to extend his house because of his growing family, the old goblin thought that sounded an excellent idea.

"But why can't you employ a builder?" he asked, reasonably.

"It's all the dust and dirt and upheaval," sighed Boxwood. "My dear wife has four little children to look after. I don't think she could cope with building work on top of everything else."

Of course, the real reason was that Boxwood couldn't be bothered to do things properly, but Millet had recently had his bathroom improved, so he knew exactly what Boxwood was talking about. He could well imagine that anyone would want to avoid unnecessary mess and fuss.

"So you'd like a spell to extend your house?" he asked.

"Yes, please," said Boxwood. "Just one extra room for the children should be enough."

"No problem," said Millet.

He went away into his study. Boxwood could hear muttering and the scratching of a pen. Minutes passed – many, many minutes. Boxwood, who was not a patient goblin at the best of times, began gnawing his knuckles in frustration. Just when Boxwood thought he would give up the whole idea, Millet reappeared, clutching a piece of parchment.

"Thanks very much," cried Boxwood, seizing it. "Sorry I can't stay longer, but I've got to fly!"

"But…" cried Millet, "I haven't told you how to use the spell.

That's most important. You could have a terrible accident."

Silly Boxwood was already halfway down the path. He didn't think he needed any further instructions. It was just a question of saying the spell, wasn't it?

Well, saying a spell is a little like using a recipe in cooking. It may be all right if you just follow the instructions, but quite a lot of common sense is needed as well. And as we know, Boxwood didn't have very much of *that*!

When Boxwood got home, Dahlia had gone to visit her mother with the children. With the house to himself, there was

Diddly-dum,
Diddly-dig,
Turn around twice,
Make my house big!
Tiddley-tum,
Tiddley-too,
Turn back again,
One room will do!

nothing to stop Boxwood trying out the spell. He looked at it carefully, but it seemed very straightforward. What could possibly go wrong?

Concentrating hard, for he knew it was important to get the words right, Boxwood read out the spell. He turned around twice after the third line and turned back again after the seventh line. Of course, if Boxwood had waited to hear what Millet had to say, he would have known that there is a special way of turning when you are doing a goblin spell. (It's quite complicated, so I won't go into it, but some of your fingers and two of your toes have to be crossed.)

The minute the spell was finished, Boxwood ran to the window to see if there was an extra room at the back of the house. But there was the garden, just as usual. A nasty thought occurred to Boxwood. What if the room had been added to the *front* of the house by mistake? He remembered that he hadn't actually told Millet where he wanted the room to be.

Boxwood poked his head out of the front door and looked left and right. What a relief! Everything looked as usual.

Boxwood took a closer look at the spell. It obviously hadn't worked. Had he said it just right? Perhaps he had got a diddly mixed up with a tiddly. The silly goblin decided to try again.

But this time, when Boxwood looked out of the front and back of the house, there was no change again. Boxwood felt very disappointed. He had looked forward to surprising Dahlia. He tried again, and again, but it was no use.

When Dahlia walked back down the road that afternoon, she certainly *was* surprised. What silly Boxwood hadn't

realised from inside the house was that the rooms had been added *on top*. Now Boxwood's house was the tallest in the village, and it quite obviously was not within goblin building regulations, which are not very strict but draw the line at six-storey houses.

Dahlia didn't need to think very hard to guess that Boxwood was responsible. It wasn't very long before that goblin knew exactly what his wife thought of him, too.

"You must go straight back to Millet and ask for the antidote," she said. "All spells can be undone, and this one must be dealt with before the authorities come round. After all, it's not exactly something you could walk past without noticing."

Boxwood didn't like having to go back to Millet and confess he had made a mistake, but he had no choice. The old goblin was not at all happy when he heard what had happened.

"It's silly young goblins like you who give magic a bad name," he said. "I'm not going to trust you to undo this mess. I shall have to come down to your house myself and sort it out. Goodness me!"

So Millet walked slowly down to Boxwood's house, which turned out to be a blessing in disguise. For there, while he was putting right the six-storey problem, he met Dahlia. She was so obviously the kind of wise, sensible goblin that should be in charge of magic that Millet asked at once if he could pass his secrets on to her. He had been looking for a long time for a young goblin to train before it was too late.

That is why Dahlia is now the most respected person in town. But she keeps her magic books well away from you-know-who!

Nursery
Rhyme
Land

Did you know that there is such a place as Nursery Rhyme Land? It's a very strange place, to be sure, with mice running up and down clocks, lost sheep, and boys and girls falling down hills and bumping their heads quite badly. There are little boys dressed in blue and little girls with curls in the middle of their foreheads. There's a crooked house, a house that Jack built, and a house that looks like a shoe – in fact, it *is* a shoe. You might see a boy in his nightshirt and one with one shoe off and one shoe on. Lots of people seem to be on

the move. One traveller is going to St Ives and another is asking the way to Norwich, while a rather silly boy is running over the hills and far away.

And just look at what they are eating! A couple divide their meat between them, a little boy pulls plums out of pies, and someone who sings for his supper is given nothing but brown bread and butter.

If you can say *all* the seventeen rhymes we've met on our brief visit to Nursery Rhyme Land, you are very clever. It's a strange place, isn't it? A very strange place indeed.

Toot! Toot!

Old Lady Loosestrife of Goblin Hall was a very light sleeper. She often tossed and turned until the early hours of the morning, before she finally drifted off to dreamland. Perhaps it was because she did not get as much sleep as she needed that Lady Loosestrife was always in a terrible temper.

Servants at Goblin Hall changed as often as the sheets. Very few of them could stand the way that Lady Loosestrife shouted at them all day long. She was never satisfied with the way that work was done. Even when the tables had been polished so that you could see every detail of your face in them, the mistress of Goblin Hall was full of fury.

"I told you to use *lavender* scented beeswax!" she would yell. "This is *lily of the valley,* and it smells horrible. Do it again, every inch!"

But no one suffered as much as Lady Loosestrife's chauffeur Buggles. Strangely enough, he had been in her employment longer than any of the other servants at the hall. His father had been chauffeur before him. And before that, his grandfather had driven Lady Loosestrife's father in a very grand carriage.

Lady Loosestrife had never taken driving lessons, and she had not the first idea about the rules of the road or the workings of a motor vehicle. But that didn't stop her. She regularly told Buggles to change into sixth gear (when he only had five) and instructed him to drive across red traffic lights. But Buggles was perfectly calm. He did what he thought was right and totally ignored Lady Loosestrife, which was just as well, for she could single-handedly have caused more traffic accidents than the rest of the inhabitants of the country put together.

More than anything else, Lady Loosestrife wanted Buggles to hoot his horn at other traffic and at passers-by. In her heart, she felt that she alone should be allowed to use the road, and other drivers and pedestrians should keep out of her way. If she had only known, other drivers and pedestrians *did* keep out of her way. They didn't want to be shouted at, and although Buggles was a very good and steady driver, who knew when he might be pushed too far and actually follow his mistress's instructions? It was not a risk worth taking.

Nevertheless, some people, of course, did have to use the roads at the same time as her ladyship. They had their livings to earn after all. Then Lady Loosestrife would scream at poor Buggles.

"Hoot at that man! He's wearing horrible trousers. It shouldn't be allowed! Hoot at that driver! How dare he have a purple car like mine? Hoot at that dog! I just know it would bite me if it could. Hoot at that policeman! His uniform buttons aren't fastened properly!"

You see, Lady Loosestrife believed that everybody's business was her business, and her business was nobody else's business at all.

Now Buggles very rarely hooted and tooted at other road users. He knew it was just as likely to cause accidents as any of Lady Loosestrife's other driving instructions. He just calmly went along at his own pace and ignored her ladyship. But that seemed to make her even crosser. One day she saw something in a catalogue that she felt would improve her chauffeur's driving enormously. It was a claxon – a kind of hooter-tooter that made an incredibly loud noise.

Next time she went out in her car, Lady Loosestrife popped the claxon into her huge handbag.

As usual, Buggles wasn't doing nearly enough hooting and tooting as far as his passenger was concerned.

"Hoot at that woman in the preposterous hat!" screamed Lady Loosestrife. "It's *too* ridiculous and much too much like one of mine. Hoot at that man with the bicycle! He looks as if he's about to wobble. Hoot at that woman with the twins! She had no business having two children at once. The very idea! Hoot at that cow. Hoot! Hoot!"

But Buggles just drove on.
Driven to distraction by his
failure to hoot and toot, Lady
Loosestrife pulled the claxon out
of her bag and opened the
window. Oh dear! What an awful
commotion! The preposterous
hat blew off in the blast, hitting
the man on the bicycle, who not
only wobbled but fell off, right in
the path of the woman with the
twins, who immediately began to
scream, upsetting the cow and
causing her to run straight down
the road and through the open
window of the fishmonger's shop.

Lady Loosestrife, oblivious to
the mayhem she was causing,

sailed on in her car, hooting her claxon at every opportunity. In this way, she blazed a trail of destruction through the countryside, and the disasters that occurred in her wake came to the notice of the local constabulary.

"That woman must be stopped," said the Chief Inspector. "I want road blocks at every junction. Poor old Buggles, it isn't his fault, but something has got to be done about Lady L."

The operation that was mounted to stop the claxon-blowing menace was bigger than any ever seen in the county. It didn't take long before Buggles, much to his mistress's disgust, pulled up at a signal from a policeman standing in the middle of the road.

"Don't stop! Don't stop!" yelled her ladyship. "He shouldn't *be* in the middle of the road. It serves him right if he's run over." And she blew her claxon several times just to show that she meant business.

But Buggles drew to a stop and wound down the window to talk to the officer.

"It's all right, Buggles old son," said the policeman. "It's not you we want. I'm afraid we're going to have to arrest Lady Loosebox there, for use of an offensive claxon and causing a breach of the peace."

I will leave you to imagine Lady Loosestrife's fury at:

1. Being taken into custody;
2. Being called Lady Loosebox;
3. Having her claxon confiscated;
4. Finding that Chief Inspectors don't follow orders from members of the public, and
5. Having to wait in a cell with a burglar, a poacher and the poacher's dog.

Lady Loosestrife told the Chief Inspector that she had every intention of buying another claxon as soon as she got home. The Chief Inspector said that as far as he was concerned, she could buy as many claxons as she liked, but she was on no account to use one. He also mentioned the fact that next time she might have to share a cell with a murderer and that no special arrangements were made in prison for members of the aristocracy.

"What, no servants?" asked Lady Loosestrife, shocked to her very marrow.

"Absolutely no servants," said the Chief Inspector, "and no caviar, champagne or Buggles."

Lady Loosestrife was silent for longer than she had been in many a long year. She agreed to be bound over to keep the peace and went rather quietly back to her car.

"Just a minute, Buggles," said the sergeant at the desk. "I've wanted to ask you something for ages. Just between you and me, how do you stand it?"

Buggles didn't pretend not to know what he meant.

"Oh, that's easy," he said. "After the first year of screaming, my hearing was so bad, I had to have a hearing aid. It has a very efficient volume control!"

The
Parrot
Problem

Miss Lavinia Blenkinsop was a very proper and particular lady. She ate her fruit with a knife and fork and always wore just the right amount of discreet jewellery. Her only regret was that the rest of her family was not so genteel. She tried not to let her friends meet them.

Then, one day, Miss Lavinia Blenkinsop had news that her Uncle Boris had died. She remembered how Uncle Boris had bounced her on his knee when she was a child. It was a shame, even though she hadn't seen the old rogue for years. Uncle Boris had been a sea captain in his youth and had sent his niece postcards from every part of the world. Rather unexpectedly, prim and proper Lavinia had had a soft spot for Uncle Boris.

A few days later, a van pulled up outside Lavinia Blenkinsop's immaculate gateway.

"Sign here, please," said the delivery man, carrying a large parcel with a big sign on it saying "This way up."

Miss Blenkinsop was very surprised, but she carried the parcel into the house and put it on the table. She saw that there was an envelope attached to it.

"Dear Miss Blenkinsop," said the letter inside, "under the terms of your uncle's last will and testament, this bird now belongs to you. It was your uncle's dearest possession, and he particularly requested that you should take good care of it."

Miss Blenkinsop smiled. A stuffed bird! How typical of Uncle Boris. Well, she needn't put it anywhere that anyone could *see* it. She undid the parcel, wondering if it would be a penguin from the North Pole or a flamingo from North Africa.

It wasn't. It was a parrot from South America – and it was alive!

Miss Lavinia Blenkinsop stared at the parrot, and the parrot stared at her.

"I'm a parrot!" he said, quite distinctly, in a loud voice.

Well, Miss Blenkinsop could see that. She had no idea how to look after a parrot, but she supposed that for Uncle Boris's sake she would have to learn. And after all, he would be a talking point. None of her prim and proper friends had parrots.

That afternoon, Miss Lavinia Blenkinsop had invited a select little party to tea. She placed the parrot in his cage prominently in the corner of the room and sat back to await reactions. She was not disappointed.

"My dear, how quaint!" said one lady in a large hat.

"What a novel idea! Isn't he a lot of trouble?" asked another.

"Not at all," said Miss Lavinia Blenkinsop. "He's as good as gold."

"Knickers!" said the parrot.

Yes, that's right. That's exactly what the parrot said, and just in case his shocked audience didn't understand him the first time, he said it again, even louder.

Miss Lavinia Blenkinsop turned pink, but she thought quickly.

"It's a Brasilian word," she said, "meaning 'Pleased to meet you.'"

The parrot made a rude noise.

"How clever he is," said his new owner. "That's a very polite term among the people of the Amazon."

Over the next few weeks, Miss B. tried to teach the parrot more polite terms, but you would be amazed how many Brasilian and Amazonian words he knew. And you would be amazed, too, if you could see how he made his owner laugh in private. It seems she had more in common with her Uncle Boris than she had realised.

So the parrot turned out not to be a problem after all. He has learnt lots of new words now – and so has Miss Lavinia Blenkinsop!

Granny
Gumdrop

Belinda climbed on to a chair and looked out of the window, as she did every day just after lunch. She held on tightly so that she didn't fall.

"Can you see her?" asked Ben.

"Yes, here she comes!" said Belinda with a giggle.

"Is she wearing her hat?"

"Yes!"

"Is she wearing her old coat?"

"Yes!"

"Has she got her boots on?"

"Yes!"

"And…?" Ben was giggling too.

"And she's got her umbrella. And it's open, it really is!"

"Silly Granny," said Ben.

The children took it in turns each day to look out of the window at the old lady. She wasn't really their granny, but they thought she looked so funny that they had nicknamed her Granny Gumdrop. They weren't usually unkind children. It was just funny the way she always dressed as if it was pouring with rain, even in the middle of the summer. Belinda and Ben had no idea that Granny Gumdrop could see them watching her as she went past.

But one day, when they were in the supermarket with their mum, the children were surprised to see a familiar figure coming round a stack of baked beans.

"It's Granny Gumdrop!" hissed Belinda, so loudly that the old lady couldn't fail to hear her.

"Why," said Granny Gumdrop, "if it isn't Hurly and Burly."

"Those aren't our names," said Ben, rather offended.

"No," said the old lady, "but Granny Gumdrop isn't *my* name. Why do you call me that, Hurly?"

Ben was younger than his sister and often alarmingly truthful.

"Because you wear a funny hat and funny clothes," he said.

"And do you want to know why I do that?" asked Granny.

"Yes," said Belinda and Ben.

"Well, why are you wearing a clown suit, Hurly? And why have you got that red hat on, Burly?" asked Granny Gumdrop.

"Because we like them," said Belinda stoutly. "Why shouldn't we wear what we like?"

"That's exactly what *I* say," said Granny Gumdrop. "I *like* my hat, and my coat, and my boots. And I specially like my old umbrella. Why shouldn't I wear what I like?"

The children looked thoughtful, and Mummy smiled and invited their new friend to tea.

"That would be a pleasure too," said Granny Gumdrop.

Don't
Be Silly,
Sally!

There was once a little girl called Sally who was not very truthful. Her mummy and daddy told her how important it was to tell the truth, but Sally didn't listen. She never told lies about things that really mattered, so she thought they were just making a fuss about nothing.

When I say that Sally didn't tell lies about things that really mattered, I mean that she wouldn't have dreamed of saying she was ill when she wasn't. And she would never have made something up about a friend or a stranger so that they appeared unkind or stupid. No, Sally's lies were about silly things. In fact, when she was a baby, her parents thought she simply had a vivid imagination, and they liked her little stories. But now that she was older, it didn't seem so funny any more.

Let me tell you the kind of thing that Sally would say.

"I've only got one sock on," she would announce at breakfast, "because I gave the other one to an elf this morning."

"Don't be silly, Sally," her mother would say. "Go and find your other sock and put it on."

"I can't eat my breakfast," the little girl would go on, "because a rabbit came in the night and borrowed my teeth!"

"Don't be silly, Sally," her father would say. "Eat up like a good girl."

Then it would be time for Sally to go to nursery.

"I don't want to wear my red coat," she would wail. "It's not a red day today. It's a blue day."

"Don't be silly, Sally!"

"There are creepy-crawly things in my boots! I can't put them on."

"Don't be silly, Sally!"

And so it went on. All day long, Sally made up stories about everything she did or saw.

If Sally saw some flowers growing by the path on her way to nursery, she would say, "I know the fairy who planted those. Her name is Annabel."

Sally's mummy and daddy hoped that their daughter was just going through a phase that would soon pass.

"She's a very imaginative little girl," said Sally's teacher. "It would be a shame to bring her down to earth too much."

"Just a little bit would be nice," said Sally's mummy. "I never know whether to believe her or not when she says something out of the ordinary."

Of course, as time went on, everyone believed Sally less and less. They got so used to her stories and inventions that they hardly listened to what she said. So when Sally came running in from the garden one day with important news, her mummy didn't pay too much attention.

"There's buzzing in the garage," cried Sally.

"Don't be silly, Sally," said her mother, automatically.

Sally went outside to play for a while. But after half an hour, she came running back inside.

"They're buzzing in and out," she said. "Like this." And she did a little dance in the middle of the sitting room.

"Don't be silly, Sally," said her mother. "No one is dancing in our garden."

"Not in the garden," said Sally. "In the garage."

"Don't be silly, Sally. The only things in the garage are the car and the bookshelves that your father started before you were

born and still hasn't finished,"
said Mummy.

So Sally went out to look again.
When she came back, she was
holding something tightly in her
striped mittens.

"Look," she said. "I caught one
of the buzzy things."

"Don't be silly, Sally. There's
nothing in your hands at all."

"Yes, there is," retorted Sally,
and she opened her arms wide.

Sally's mummy carried on with
her work, but a second or two
later she quite distinctly heard a
buzzing sound. It was a bee.

Then Mummy shut the doors
and windows and called Daddy

down from his workroom.

"There's a swarm of bees in our garage," she said. "Sally discovered them."

Daddy looked doubtful for a moment, but Mummy and Sally spoke together.

"No," they said, "it's *true!*"

Some men came to take away the bees before they stung anyone.

Mummy and Daddy listen a little more carefully to what Sally says these days. Perhaps that's why Sally doesn't make things up quite so often – except when she doesn't want to wear blue socks, of course. Then those naughty elves *will* come and steal them!

Titles in this Series include

The Curious Kitten
The Enchanted Treasure
The Sleepy Teddy Bear
The Clever Little Rabbit
The First Little Fairy
The Elegant Elf
The Friendly Pig
The Busy Baker
The Smiling Star
The Forgetful Squirrel